NEMO MEETS
THE EMPEROR

By Laura Bannon

Illustrated by
Katherine Evans

ALBERT WHITMAN & CO. CHICAGO

To Abigail Trueblood
who was born in Ethiopia, by the artist
who visited her father and mother there
one winter.

THE LION OF ETHIOPIA

In the highlands of Africa, a small brown boy gathered hay from a field. Nemo, for that was his name, tied the hay into a bundle.

As he worked he talked to his little burro, Abu. Of course he said his words in the language of Ethiopia because he was an Ethiopian boy.

"That's a mighty big load of hay, Abu," he told his burro. "We'll rest ourselves before we carry it home."

Nemo's black eyes traveled to the valley below, to the city of Addis Ababa.

Tops of the tallest buildings pushed out of the mist that filled the valley's hollows. That large roof down there was the palace of the Emperor.

Nemo sat down on a rock and gazed at it with day-dreaming eyes.

"Some day, Abu, I'm going inside that palace. I'm going to walk right up that long red carpet they talk about. And do you know who I'm going to meet at the other end of that red carpet?"

The burro moved nearer to Nemo.

4

"The Emperor will be sitting there, Abu. Sitting in a gold chair, just waiting to meet me. The Emperor of all Ethiopia!"

The burro's velvet lips nibbled at Nemo's brown head. Except for a small tuft of hair, his head was shaved as smooth as a nut.

Nemo giggled and held his hand over the tuft. "What are you trying to do, Abu? Eat my topknot?"

He jumped to his feet and boosted the hay to the burro's back. Then he doubled over laughing at the sight of Abu, lost in the bundle of hay.

"You just fade away under this big load, Abu. Are you too covered up to see your way?"

Nimble little Abu could see well

enough. He started down the hill, picking his way between the rocks to the *tukul* that was Nemo's home.

Mama Zoadie sat by the door of the round thatched hut. Her slim fingers flew over a loom, weaving the cotton cloth that made their clothes.

"Look, Mama," called Nemo. "Abu is lost. My bundle of hay walks on his four legs."

A full smile chased the worry from Mama Zoadie's face. "That's a fine big load, Nemo. What would I do without your help? As soon as you eat, we will take the hay and the wood I have split down to the market."

Nemo tore a piece from a giant pancake, a pancake as big as the circle he could make with his two arms.

6

He dipped the piece into a sauce called *watt*. He smacked his lips as he ate. Even when Mama had no meat to put into it, she could make the *watt* taste good. It was so hot with red peppers it pushed tears into his eyes.

"With such a big load of hay to sell, maybe today we can buy some mutton for the *watt*," he suggested.

"That would taste good, my son. But it is better to save a little money for the time of the big rains if we can do so. I think I must ask for work down in the city."

Nemo ate in silence. Maybe some day he could get a job, too, he thought. It might happen that he would be sent with a message to the Emperor. He would walk right up that red ——

"Come, Nemo. We'll go to the market now." Mama had the wood loaded on her back.

Nemo slapped Abu awake. Soon they were zigzagging down the steep path to the main road.

A string of camels raised the dust of the road with their great plopping feet. They held their heads high and seemed not to mind their heavy loads of wood and fur.

The road was crowded with mules, fat-tailed sheep, and two-wheeled carts.

At the market, Mama Zoadie called to the peddler who sold monkey-fur rugs.

"*Tan esteling*, greetings," she said. "Do you know of someone who needs

a servant? I must find some work."

The peddler called back, "No, but I will keep an ear open for you."

Mama knew many of the people who squatted with their wares on the cobblestones. She sold her wood and bought barley, red peppers and onions. The money from the load of hay bought a ball of butter wrapped in cornhusks.

Wherever they went Mama Zoadie asked for work, but found none.

At last they stopped at the stall for fancy goods. They looked at the bright beads and anklets and the silver-mounted saddles for the highborn.

The young woman who sold trinkets wagged her head as she talked.

10

Her hair was well buttered and divided into neat furrows. She told about seeing the Emperor on the street.

Nemo was all ears.

"The Emperor was elegant in his black cape," the woman said. "His servant held a red umbrella over him."

"He is a good Emperor," said Mama Zoadie. "And yet the times are hard. I am not able to save any money for the time of the big rains. If only I could find work."

"You might ask for work with the American family at Casa Inches," said the woman. "I hear that the nursemaid for their little daughter has left them."

This was good news. "Come, Nemo,"

said Mama Zoadie. "We will hurry home and get ourselves ready to ask for the job tomorrow."

Mama Zoadie and Nemo prodded their little burro along the path that led up to their *tukul*.

The sun slid down the sky and went to bed behind Mount Entoto, pulling the daylight after it.

Hyenas, that had slept all day in their hiding places in the hills, came out to call to each other. The countryside rang with their drawn out, "Whroo-oo-ee-eeh."

Soon they would be slinking down the ravines to the streets of Addis Ababa. All night they would prowl the dark to gnaw bones and gobble scraps.

When hyenas are on the prowl, it is

best to keep out of their way. Even Abu knew that. He quickened his mincing steps and soon the little family was safely home.

The next morning Nemo awoke before daylight. Mama Zoadie was already up. She laughed at Nemo when he tried to rub the sleep from his eyes.

"Jump out of your goatskin, sleepyhead. I want to roll it with mine to take with us."

They ate what was left of the pancakes and *watt*. They loaded the goatskins and Mama's loom on Abu. When the day was still new and filled with mist, they were on their way.

A short distance down the hill from the *tukul* they stopped. Here the brook, tired of tumbling on its way,

14

rested in a quiet place and formed a pool.

"Now we will make ourselves clean," said Mama Zoadie.

Nemo slipped off his long shirt and sat on a rock in his skin. He watched while Mama washed the shirt and her dress in the proper way.

She piled them together in the pool and trod on them. She had danced this washday jig so many times that she did it easily and well. Her strong feet stamped the clothes in quick rhythm.

By the time the sun began to climb the sky, the clothes were stretched smooth on a rock to dry.

Nemo and Mama washed themselves until they shone like brown leaves in the rain.

Mama combed her thick frizzy hair with a wooden comb and neatly tied a red, square cloth over it. Her head looked like a big pincushion.

Cool and clean, they were on their way again by the time their neighbors were building their morning fires. Smoke seeped through the roofs of the *tukuls* that dotted the hills.

Hopefully, Mama and Nemo pat-patted along in their bare feet, on their way to the Americans' home.

Nemo had never before been farther than the market place. The streets beyond were a strange world to him.

He and Mama had to look sharp to keep Abu and his load from being run over by the automobiles.

The hot white sun beat down upon them. Nemo flapped the front of his shirt to fan himself.

At last they came to the high wall that hid the Americans' house.

"What do you want?" asked the guard who stood by the gate.

The worry look was on Mama Zoadie's face. She answered in a small voice, "I want to speak to the American mama. I am told she is in need of a nursemaid."

The guard called to the Number One servant boy. Number One Boy told them to leave their burro outside and follow him.

The house looked big enough for a hundred families. The many openings were covered with glass.

Number One Boy twisted a white knob on the door to open it. How cold and slippery the floor inside felt to bare feet that were used to the soft warm earth.

Nemo peeped out from behind Mama's skirt. He stretched his neck to watch the pale lady coming down the long hall.

Mama Zoadie bowed low and said, *"Tan esteling."*

The lady began to talk with the strange English words that were hard to understand. Number One Boy helped by changing the words into the language used by Ethiopians.

Had Mama Zoadie ever served as nursemaid? Had she ever worked for a foreign family?

No, no! Mama's answers were No.

The worry look spread all over poor little Mama Zoadie.

Nemo felt frightened. He wanted to take Mama's hand and leave the big cold house. He wanted to go home to their own friendly *tukul*.

"Abby, come here, dear," called the lady.

A small girl came running down the hall. She was all pink and white like the tiny mountain flower that pops up after the rain. Her long smooth hair gleamed like sunshine.

Nemo had never seen anything like her before. Why was she so white?

"This is my daughter, Abigail Thomas," said Mrs. Thomas. "We call her Abby."

Abby fixed her wide blue eyes on Nemo. She walked slowly up to him and smiled.

Nemo smiled from ear to ear.

Mama Zoadie smiled.

Mrs. Thomas smiled and talked to Number One Boy. He explained her words to Mama Zoadie.

"She says that her little girl likes you. You and your boy are very neat and clean. You may stay and learn to be a nursemaid."

It was settled. Before nightfall Mama and Nemo had moved into the servants' quarters in the great yard back of the house. Abu was tied to a nearby tree.

The first days at the American house were worry-days.

These foreign people had such strange ways of doing things. And they must have everything done in their own way. Nemo felt sure that Mama Zoadie's ways were best.

Mrs. Thomas asked Mama to wash Abby's clothes. Nemo carried sticks of wood to build a fire in the little stove in the bathroom.

Then Mrs. Thomas showed them how to make a miracle. When a knob was turned, a waterfall of warm water came out of the wall. She gave Mama a bar of soap and left her to wash the clothes.

Mama Zoadie was pleased with the soap. She never could afford it for herself. But she knew how to use it.

She made a nice pool of warm water

24

in the bathtub. She put the clothes into it and rubbed plenty of soap on them.

Then she lifted her skirts and climbed into the tub. She trod on the clothes with her bare feet. Great puffs of bubbles squeezed up around her ankles.

"I'll help you," said Nemo.

Together Mama and Nemo jigged on the clothes in a kind of soapsuds dance.

Nemo giggled himself weak.

"Sh-sh-sh." Mama Zoadie hushed him. "When in the house, we must keep the laugh inside us."

Nemo tried to do so but he got so filled up with the laugh that it burst out suddenly in a big snort.

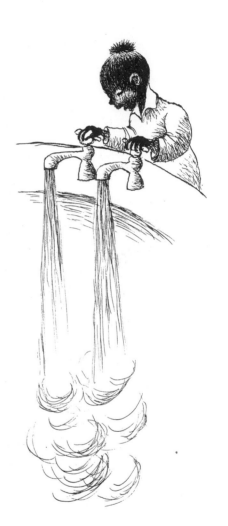

Mrs. Thomas stuck her head through the door and cried, "No, no. You don't wash clothes with your feet." She shook her head and pointed to make sure Mama Zoadie understood.

Not wash clothes with feet! How else?

Mrs. Thomas showed Mama how American clothes are washed with the hands.

"Yes, yes." Mama Zoadie bowed. She could learn to do things the American way as well as the sensible way.

Mrs. Thomas crooked her finger at Nemo. The finger said to follow her. She had a job for him.

She handed him a can with a long spout. She showed him the plants that stood inside the house in pots, like

little prisoners. She wriggled her fingers like rain.

Nemo grinned his big grin. "Yes, yes." He understood. He just about bowed his topknot off. He was to bring the drink of rain to the little prisoners.

He went to the well in the back yard and filled the can with water. First he would rain on the plants that stood together in a corner of the big room. He would do it just like real rain.

Nemo stood on a chair and held the can high. He swished a fine spray back and forth across all the plants.

This was fun. The whole corner of the room was nice and damp, just as if it had really been rained on.

"No, no, Nemo!" There was Mrs.

Thomas shaking her head as Abu does when a flea gets into his ear.

"Like this," she said and tilted the can over each plant separately.

"Yes, yes." Nemo bowed and grinned. He was a smart boy. He, too, could do things the American way as well as the sensible way. After that each little plant had its own small rain.

Nemo learned just what he must do when Mrs. Thomas said to him, "Spraythebedrooms."

At once he became a great hunter with a spray gun. The fleas were hyenas.

He hunted down the little black ones that hid between the sheets. He crawled into the dark cave under the beds and slew the big ones that

29

waited there for the night to come.

The beds stood up on four legs like animals. Just to look at them made Nemo want to laugh. He knew that was not the sensible place to sleep. At night you should roll up in a goatskin and lie on the floor where there is no fear of falling.

Nemo's happiest hours were spent watching over Miss Abby.

He made her laugh by turning somersaults. Or he would make himself into a monkey with long white hair. He did this by peeping through the swish part of the fly swisher.

He carried the fly swisher because Mrs. Thomas told him that flies carry bad germs. If they lit on Miss Abby, they might make her sick.

All the flies that Nemo saw came buzzing up empty-footed. But he swished them away from Miss Abby anyway, just because her mother said to do it.

English words were easy to learn from Miss Abby because she was just learning them herself. She pointed to the water and said "Wa-wa."

Nemo also learned to name her clothes just as Miss Abby named them —dwess, sooes, and toat.

He taught Miss Abby to say Ethiopian words. *"Tan esteling,"* he would say.

"Tan es'eling," she would say after him.

Being a sensible boy, Nemo soon learned the reasons for things. The

Thomas family had lost the brown-
ness from their skins because they
washed themselves too much.

Poor little Miss Abby was palest
because she got scrubbed all over
every day. Her face and hands got
extra washings besides.

She was not to blame. She screamed
and wanted to play with Nemo in-
stead of being washed.

Next best to playing with Miss
Abby, Nemo liked to carry messages
for Mrs. Thomas to other foreign
houses. He would ride off, sitting on
the back end of Abu.

The note in his hand would ask a for-
eigner to come and drink up tea. Or
it might say that Mrs. Thomas had
decided to go and drink up their tea.

On these trips, Nemo always kept an eye out for the Emperor. He might whiz by in a big automobile. But he never did. Or perhaps he would walk while a servant held a red umbrella over him. But he never did.

One morning Mrs. Thomas gave money to Number One Boy to give to Nemo.

"She says that you make a good messenger boy," he told Nemo. "But you should wear something better than your old shirt. You are to take this money to a tailor and have him make a shirt and pants for you."

"Shirt and pants, too?" A grin spread over Nemo's face. It was still there when he came to the market place where the tailors sat at sewing

machines. The grin lasted all the way through the stitching of the shirt.

Nemo whisked off the old shirt and carefully pulled on the stiff, white, new shirt.

The tailor made his feet go fast. The needle zinged along the tight pant legs.

Suddenly a beautiful thought popped into Nemo's head. His grin changed to a look of wonder.

Now he knew why Mrs. Thomas had decided that the old shirt wasn't good enough. She was going to send him with a note to the Emperor.

The instant the last thread was snapped, Nemo jumped into the pants and hurried home.

Mrs. Thomas said he looked fine in

his new suit. But she said nothing at all about sending him with a note to the Emperor.

One day a man on horseback brought a note to the big house.

Yasin, who drove the Thomas car, told Number One Boy, who told Mama Zoadie, who told Nemo, that the note came from the Emperor.

The Emperor was giving a party for all the foreign children in Addis Ababa. Even though Abby was not quite three years old, she was invited.

Mama Zoadie was sent to buy a new fly swisher and a dress for herself. Each child should have her nurse to watch over her.

Miss Abby would wear the beautiful blue dress sent from America. Mama

Zoadie starched and ironed her little petticoats and bonnet until they were as smooth and stiff as the petals of a lily.

Nemo taught Miss Abby to bow and say, *"Tan esteling*, Your Majesty."

The day of the party, Yasin polished the car. He put a bouquet of flowers on top of the radiator.

Mrs. Thomas dressed up in a new white dress, a wide hat, and coverings for her hands and arms.

Nemo learned a new English word when Miss Abby called the coverings "glubs."

Nemo washed himself at the well and put on the new suit.

Mama Zoadie, carrying her fly swisher, climbed into the car with

Abby. Mrs. Thomas followed her. Nemo stood ready with a big grin on his face.

Yasin, who wore a fresh flower in his nostril, looked straight ahead and started the car. Off they went to the Emperor's party without Nemo.

Nemo ran to the garden and cried on the sleeve of his new shirt.

Who was calling his name? Number One Boy was shouting, "Mrs. Thomas wants you to come at once. Miss Abby won't go to the party without you."

Nemo ran to the street.

Miss Abby was screaming her face red. But she stopped when Nemo climbed in the front seat beside Yasin.

Nemo's grin almost split his face in two. The grin lasted all the way

through the busy streets to the palace gate. The tall guard on each side of the gate was made taller by his high turban.

Yasin drove right through the gate and on between the long row of trees up to the palace.

Nemo was still grinning.

Mrs. Thomas got out. Mama Zoadie got out with Miss Abby.

"You wait outside the gate in the car, Nemo," said Mrs. Thomas.

Yasin turned the car around and drove back through the gate.

Nemo's grin dissolved in tears that streamed down his face and wetted the front of his new shirt. Yasin left the car and lost himself in the crowd. Nemo sat alone and sobbed.

No use to hope or pretend. He knew now that he would never walk up the red carpet to meet the Emperor. If only he could just watch Miss Abby do it.

Nemo looked up at the high palace wall. Still higher up, a buzzard roosted in a tree and looked down on the palace grounds.

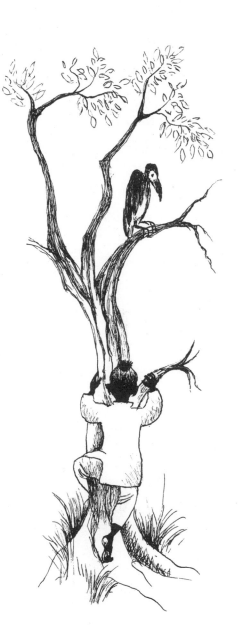

Nemo jumped out of the car. He was good at climbing trees. In no time at all the buzzard was gone, and it was Nemo who roosted in the tree and looked down on the children's party.

His eyes hunted among the bright colored umbrellas for Miss Abby. What a crowd of foreign boys and girls! Servants in fancy coats carried trays of little cakes to the children.

41

There was Mama Zoadie talking to a group of nursemaids. Her fly swisher kept up a lively swishing as she talked. But she was not swishing flies off Miss Abby because Abby wasn't with her.

Where was Miss Abby? Nemo couldn't see her anywhere. What if little Miss Abby got lost in all that crowd!

Nemo could see one end of the red carpet. The foreign women were walking over to it with their sons and daughters. They stood in a row on each side of the carpet.

Oh, oh! Now Mama Zoadie, and Mrs. Thomas too, were running around the bushes like hens without heads. They were hunting for Miss Abby. That was as plain as the ear on a mule.

A man in a green and gold coat boomed out, "Madame John Johnson from Sweden and her son, Kurt Johnson."

A big woman walked up the red carpet with her son. They were washed white.

There was Mrs. Thomas 'way over beyond the bushes, looking for Abby. Mama Zoadie was crying in her lap with her arms around her head. Miss Abby must be stolen.

Nemo couldn't just sit there. Somehow he must help find Miss Abby. He slid and tumbled from the tree.

As he ran to the palace gate he heard the big voice boom out another strange-sounding name. Miss Abby's name might be called at any time.

44

"Nemo, Nemo," a small voice sobbed.

There was Abby. The guards had stopped her at the gate. Nemo paid no attention to their babbling. He grabbed Abby's tiny hand and ran with her into the palace grounds. He would take her to Mrs. Thomas.

But where was Mrs. Thomas? She must be off somewhere hunting for Abby.

The big voice boomed out again, "Madame William Thomas from America and her daughter, Abigail Patricia Thomas."

There was only one thing to do. Sensible Nemo did it. While everyone watched, even the Emperor, Nemo wiped the tears from Miss Abby's face

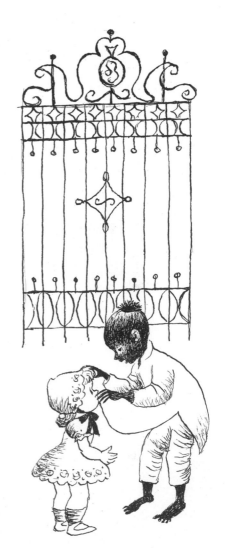

with his shirt tail. He straightened her bonnet.

"Remember, Miss Abby," he whispered. "*Tan esteling*, Your Majesty."

With his topknot bobbing, Nemo walked with Miss Abby up the long red carpet.

At the other end of the carpet the dignified Emperor sat in a gold chair. His sad dark eyes watched Nemo and Abby marching up to him.

Tiny Miss Abby bowed low. "*Tan es'eling*, Your Majes'y," she piped.

The Emperor smiled. He stood up

and shook hands with Miss Abby. *"Tan esteling,* Miss Abigail Patricia Thomas."

Nemo bowed until his head touched the carpet. His shirt tail flapped in the breeze.

"What is your name?" The Emperor asked Nemo.

"Nemo, Your Majesty."

"You are a good friend of Miss Abigail?"

"Yes, Your Majesty. And I am also a good messenger boy and very sensible."

"When you are older, Nemo, perhaps you can speak English well enough to be a messenger boy for the palace."

Nemo's eyes popped and he grinned his big grin. "Yes, Your Majesty. I can already say wa-wa, dwess, sooes, toat and glubs. And I can also say a big word, too. Spraythebedrooms."

Then Nemo found out something he never knew before. An Emperor can laugh aloud! This one did.

"That is a very good beginning," the Emperor told Nemo.